To J, for her deep engagement and trust, and for her love of climbing trees, just like the children. — BA

We are deeply grateful to Paula Holmes for her generous support, without which the beautiful Italian printing of this book would not have been possible. Thank you, Paula, for always valuing what is most valuable. — ELB

Enchanted Lion gratefully acknowledges generous support
from the Swedish Arts Council for the translation.

About Unruly

This is the fourth book to be published under Unruly, Enchanted Lion's imprint of picture books for teenagers and adults. We launched Unruly because we believe that we never age out of pictures and visual stories, and that we long for them across our lives.

In these pages, Stridsberg's poetic text moves with and against Alemagna's moody, heart-fathoming art in a beautiful, philosophical ode to the infinities of childhood as expressed through the metaphor of the park—that forest in the city where time and all of the ordinary rules no longer hold.

www.enchantedlion.com

Enchanted Lion Books would like to thank Lukas Bacho, Emma Vitoria,
and Dasha Tolstikova for their contributions to the English-language translation
and visual sequencing of the book.

First English-language edition published in 2024 by Enchanted Lion Books,
248 Creamer Street, Studio 4, Brooklyn, NY 11231
English-language edition published in agreement with Koja Agency
Copyright © 2021 by Sara Stridsberg for the text
Copyright © 2021 by Beatrice Alemagna for the illustrations
Copyright © 2024 by B.J. Woodstein for the English-language translation
Originally published in Sweden as *Vi går till parken* by Mirando Bok
Design of the English-language edition by Dasha Tolstikova

All rights reserved under International and Pan-American Copyright Conventions
A CIP record is on file with the Library of Congress

ISBN 978-1-59270-407-1

Printed in Italy by Socièta Editoriale Grafiche AZ srl
Distributed throughout the world by ABRAMS, New York

First Printing

SARA STRIDSBERG
BEATRICE ALEMAGNA

We Go to the Park

Translated from Swedish
by B.J. Woodstein

an
Enchanted Lion Book
NEW YORK

Some say we come from the stars,
that we're made of stardust,
that we once swirled into the world
from nowhere.

We don't know.
So we go to the park.

The park is a forest in the city.
It is the land beyond.
In the park, anything can happen.
Sometimes so much happens that
the whole world turns upside down.
Sometimes nothing happens at all.

Either way, we just want to go to the park.

Here in the park, the trees
stretch their branches
towards the sky like old hands.

The trees have stood here for a thousand years
and they plan to stand here longer still.

We are like the trees: we don't want to leave either.

We don't want to go back to where we were before.
Where there are buses and shops, trains and
elevators, escalators, cranes, and sidewalks.
To where everything is so big there's no room
for it inside of us.

When we sit under the enormous flowers,
not even the rain can reach us.
Some flowers are big as our heads.

Out of the blue, there might be someone in the park who we didn't know existed.

Standing next to a tree trunk,
there might be a creature
in a yellow raincoat with wild hair,
who smells like lightning and isn't
scared of anything, who shouts:
"Come on!"
"Where are we going?"
"Nowhere."
"Who are we?"
"No one in particular."

The wind is the breath of a dragon.
We let it take us where it will.

We come up with things that no one
has come up with before.
There are no rules in the universe.

"Goodbye, city!"
"Goodbye, world!"
"Goodbye, everyone!"

We swear that we're never going home again.
"Do you hear us?"
"We're never going home again."

We hide under the flowers or behind the big trees.
Because when we come back to the park again,
it might be too late.

In just a second, everything we love might be gone.

It can take ages to get back there
once we've been chased away.
"Can we go to the park, Mom?"
"Later."
"How about now?"
"In a little while."
"When will we go?"
"Later."
"Okay. When's later?"
Later can mean light-years from now.

By then, everyone and everything might have
swirled away to somewhere else.

The girl in the yellow raincoat has disappeared
between the trees, and all that's left
is the lingering, slightly sad smell of lightning
and wild hair.

Sometimes it feels as if all of life
is made up of longing.

A dizzying lack of someone
to swing and swoosh beside.

But there are other things, not just girls
in yellow raincoats.
The birdlike old ladies on benches exist,
and the friendly drunks exist, as do
ice cream cones and cotton candy and rainbows.

And if no one else wants to play, there's always a little bird or an ant with six legs to be with. It's better to do something alone than to run after those who don't want to.

Some say we come from the stars.
We don't really know,
but we go to the park anyway.

Time lurches ahead. Leaves fall from the trees. Suns rise and set. As quickly as everything disappears, suddenly it's back, without us understanding what happened.

A yellow raincoat swooshes past as swiftly
as a butterfly. There's a laugh nearby.
And the smell of something wild and warm in the wind.
Lightning strikes the heart once more.

"Hi again."
"Hi yourself."
"What's happening now?"
"We shall see."

We don't know much about what will happen next...
just that the swings here launch us straight into the sky.

And when darkness falls, we go home.
We follow our parents wherever they lead.
We are still so small in the world
and we don't want to be without them.

Then the park belongs to the trees and the birds
and the black rats once more.

The clouds settle down to sleep on the ground.

From high above, it looks as though
someone has swept the whole playground
clean with a huge broom and made all
the people disappear.

But it's just night coming on.

Tomorrow we'll be back.
And then anything can happen.